Radio Alert

JOHN ESCOTT

Illustrated by Trevor Stubley

PUFFIN BOOKS

Puffin Books, Penguin Books Ltd, Harmondsworth, Middlesex, England
Viking Penguin Inc., 40 West 23rd Street, New York, New York 10010, U.S.A.
Penguin Books Australia Ltd, Ringwood, Victoria, Australia
Penguin Books Canada Ltd, 2801 John Street, Markham, Ontario, Canada L3R 1B4
Penguin Books (N.Z.) Ltd, 182–190 Wairau Road, Auckland 10, New Zealand

First published by Hamish Hamilton Children's Books 1984
Published in Puffin Books 1987

Printed and bound in Great Britain by
Cox & Wyman Ltd, Reading
Typeset in Baskerville

398712
JS

1 A Special Island

The news jingle burst into life, triggered off by the radio alarm which Donald had set the night before.

"Roundbay Radio – News!"

He turned over and stuffed his head under the pillow. The walls of the bedroom were plastered with stickers and posters advertising Roundbay Radio, and beside his bed on a wide shelf was a jumble of tapes, earphones and a microphone.

The red figures on the digital clock part of the radio moved on to seven three. The local news, read by Greg Wills, began.

I

"Last night's gales caused severe damage to properties in the Roundbay Radio area. A number of trees have been blown down and, on the seafront, several beach huts have been wrecked . . . "

Donald pulled the bedclothes off and hung over the side of the bed. He put his hands on the floor and carefully rolled on to the carpet where he lay, curled like a snake, for several minutes.

"Donald!" His mother's voice floated up the stairs. "You'd better get this breakfast down you, time's marching on."

Ten minutes later and Donald was cycling up to the cliff top.

There was still a strong wind and the beach below was littered with rubbish which had been washed ashore. Heel Bay – shaped as its name suggested, like the heel of a shoe – was full of

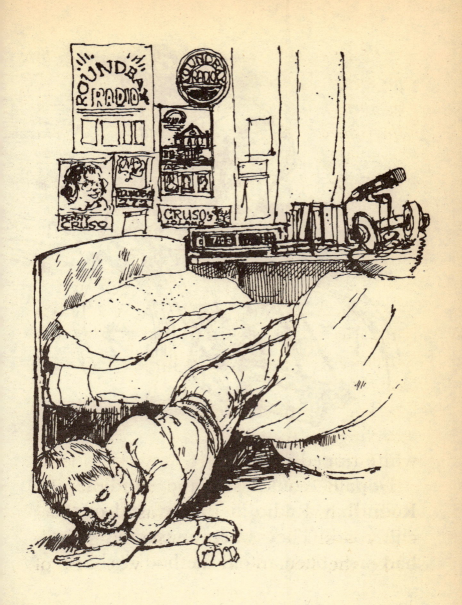

white-tipped waves.

Donald could see the studios of
Roundbay Radio at the far end of the
cliff road. They were housed in what
had once been an old methodist chapel.

Months before the local station had gone on the air, he had watched the alterations going on – studios being built and soundproofed, the old chapel porch becoming the glass-fronted reception area.

He had followed its progress with interest, never dreaming that he would become involved with it. But then, two months ago, he had won a Roundbay Radio competition and with it his own

part to play in the local station.

A horn blared and Donald swerved on to the grass verge as a car swept by.

"Watch it!" Donald shouted, then suddenly recognised the tall figure of Mr Munford. The narrow-faced man with thinning hair gave no sign of having seen him, staring straight ahead across the steering wheel.

Donald muttered beneath his breath and manoeuvred his bike back on to the road. He didn't like Mr Edgar Munford, Programme Controller of Round-bay Radio.

He glanced at his watch. Seven thirty-two, but not much farther to go. There were not many people about. Down below, workmen were inspecting the damage on the seafront.

At the other end, where the sand curved round and gradually turned to shingle, the small solitary figure of a girl moved along the sea's edge. She was carrying a sack and picking things up every few metres.

"Bit cold for beachcombing," Donald said to himself as he remounted his bike.

By seven-forty, he had parked his bike at the rear of the Roundbay Radio building and climbed the stairs to the main office.

Tracy Wills sat outside Studio C watching her father through a glass panel. Greg Wills saw Donald and waved. He was talking into a microphone which sprouted like a flower at the end of a long stem in front of him. Donald waved back.

Tracy yawned and rubbed her eyes. Donald knew she would have been up at least two hours because she came in with her father in time for his early morning news and music programme.

"You look like a tortoise at the end of winter," Donald told her as she came across.

They walked through rows of empty desks which stretched back to glass-

panelled offices at the rear. It was quiet now but in an hour there would be more people bustling about.

At one desk, however, sat a small pretty young woman with short-cropped dark hair and large owl-eyes glasses.

Penny Cruso looked up and smiled. "Morning, Tracy. Hallo, Donald. Now where's Sam? Overslept again, do you think?"

"He'll be here," Donald said.

He noticed her glancing anxiously towards one of the glass-panelled offices where Mr Munford's tall figure stood framed in the doorway. The Programme Controller's eyebrows were drawn together in a frown and he was looking directly at Penny.

Moments later, Sam arrived. He was gasping for breath having run all the

way from home. "Sorry I'm . . . late. I
. . ."

"Overslept," Donald, Tracy and
Penny said.

Penny grinned. "You'd better catch your breath before I give you anything to read. Come on, it's almost news time."

The four of them went across to Studio B.

Donald could feel Mr Munford watching them. The Programme Controller's eyes seemed to burn holes in the back of Donald's head.

(Opening music . . .)

"Welcome ashore to Cruso's Island. Your own, very special desert island . . ."

(Music fades.)

"Hallo, this is Penny Cruso and we're here again for another hour on the Island . . ."

(Sound of sea and gulls . . .)

"It's three minutes past eight on a Saturday morning, and I hope you're all wide enough awake to listen to the music, and the letters,

12

stories and poems you've been sending in. But first let's say hallo to our shipwrecked crew – Tracy, Sam and Donald. Hallo, crew."

"Hallo!"

"Mm, well they're in good voice, aren't they? How about our resident parrot on the Island – Friday. Hallo, Friday."

(Loud parrot squawk followed by flapping of wings.)

"Well we begin, as usual, with a record. Who's it for, Tracy?"

"It's for Lisa Chambers who is seven years old today. Lisa lives in Garden Drive, Auksea. Her Mum and Dad sends lots of love."

"Thank you, Tracy. And happy birthday from all of us here, Lisa. The record is The King's New Clothes, sung by Danny Kaye."

(Fade in record . . .)

2   *Beach Find*

THE BEACH SLOPED steeply downwards
and the tideline made a trail for Zoe to
follow. She did so, her small sack in one
hand, stooping and gathering the frag-
ments of shell and cuttlefish, smooth
chunks of pale driftwood, coloured glass
and dented cans. Occasionally, a wave
sent her scuttling higher up the beach
or the grey scum in a rock pool soaked
her shoe.

Zoe was choosy, sifting the items
carefully. The shape mattered, she
knew that much. And it had to be
interesting, the man had said. Interesting? How could junk be interesting?
Well, if the bloke was daft enough to *pay*

for it, Zoe wasn't going to argue.

She was a moving speck against the backdrop of the cliff face, gulls circling overhead, some swooping and scavenging on the beach. The wind had died down a little and there were some blue cracks in the battle-ship grey clouds overhead.

It had been a week of heavy storms – more like December than April – all building up to last night's gale which had seemed to rip the heart out of the little town of Auksea.

It had kept Zoe awake as she listened to the slates rattling and sliding on the roof above her bedroom. Her grand-father had slept through it all, snoring loudly in his room along the hall.

Zoe had come to stay with the old man while her parents were away. It wasn't the first time, and she enjoyed the visits. She liked the little town of Auksea with its steep hills, its narrow rambling streets. She and her parents lived in a city, a hundred miles from the sea.

She paused in her collecting, straightening her back. Farther away, where the concrete promenade began, she could see some of the results of the storm's damage. Several beach huts had been battered and a tree hung at a crazy angle on the cliff side, its trunk split.

She moved on – and immediately kicked something hard.

"Ow!" Zoe massaged her toe through her canvas shoe. "Hell's buckets!" It was an expression of her grandfather's. Whenever she came to stay with the old man she found herself speaking like him after a few days.

She snatched angrily at the object in
the sand; a bright orange metal con-
tainer, a bit like a baked bean tin but
with strange writing on it. Foreign
writing? It looked foreign. It was a good
bright colour – a gaudy orange – and
the man liked bright colours.

She dropped it into the sack and
moved on.

After a while, she climbed up on to a stone jetty and went along to the end where she sat down. Her feet dangled over the side. Beneath, the sea washed against weed-covered pilings, sucking and slurping like an ill-mannered diner.

On the promenade, workmen were clearing the storm damage, loading the back of a small green truck with what was left of the beach huts. They worked steadily, the wind blowing their hair and flapping their overalls against their legs.

On the beach, a man was fishing. His rod leaned against a v-shaped rest which had been stuck into the sand, the tip of the rod bowing and swaying against the tug of the waves. The man was sitting on a canvas stool and a transistor radio stood on the sand beside him. Zoe caught snatches of music and voices.

" . . . *and that was* The King's New Clothes. *Now Donald's going to read us one of your letters . . .*"

Zoe pulled herself to her feet, picking up the sack. She walked back along the jetty.

"Hey!"

Zoe looked up, thinking somebody had called her. But it was the fisherman waving to two workmen, calling them over. He was looking at something in the sand and holding a handkerchief to his face.

The workmen passed by Zoe and some minutes later she had drawn level with the little trio as they stooped over the object in the sand. All three were now holding handkerchiefs to their faces. Zoe suddenly realised why.

"Ugh, what a pong!" she said to

herself, screwing up her nose. Some
dead fish? It was impossible to see as
the men were near the water's edge and
Zoe had moved up the steep sands now.
She moved on, away from the smell.

A steep zig-zag path led to the cliff top. It curled round giving unexpected glimpses of Heel Bay, Auksea and the other smaller towns which sheltered against the hills.

The figures on the beach became tiny, the truck on the promenade a green toy. The two workmen and the fisherman were making their way across to the promenade, Zoe noticed. The fishing rod seemed forgotten.

There was an unpleasant taste in Zoe's mouth which hadn't been there earlier and traces of the smell from the beach seemed to have invaded her nose and insides. The climb proved harder work than usual. On the verge at the top of the cliff was a seat. Zoe sank thankfully on to it. Her mouth felt dry as chalk.

Aaron Kinray rose early, the habit of a
lifetime, but Zoe had beaten him to it
this morning, he noticed. The old man
had come into the kitchen to find the
remains of Zoe's cornflakes on the
draining board and a note – *Gone to the
beach* – beside it.

Mr Kinray went down the curling staircase which led from his flat to the shop below. He was enormously fat. Thick folds of pink flesh burst out over his shirt collar.

St Mary's church clock struck half-past eight in the distance. Mr Kinray nodded to himself. It was an every-thing-is-as-it-should-be nod and he did it each time he heard the church clock striking.

Mr Kinray was 'responsible' for St Mary's clock as almost every Auksea person knew. It was he who wound it each evening, he who changed the hour when British Summertime began or ended. Some people called the clock 'Kinray's Timepiece', but not to his face.

Kinray's Bookshop was one of the oldest bookstores in the area and had

the familiar musty smell which all second-hand bookshops suffer from. Mr Kinray wrinkled his nose with pleasure as he came down the stairs.

He unfurled the blind on the door and turned the sign to OPEN. Near the door was a desk with a red leather top and, behind it, an ancient swivel chair into which Mr Kinray now sank.

The shop window was a large bay, divided off from the shop by a net curtain. Mr Kinray pulled the curtain to one side and checked the clock on St Mary's square tower. The church was at the top of the narrow street and his chair was positioned so that he was able to see it without getting up.

He smiled, remembering Zoe. She had pestered the life out of him to be taken up to see the insides of St Mary's clock, have the workings explained.

"When you're older," he had told her. "The steps are tricky and I don't want your mother and father blaming me for letting you break your neck."

Yet he knew the girl was becoming impatient, especially on that last visit before Christmas when she'd kept on and on about it. Almost as if she believed there was something *extra*-special, something magical even, about the clock.

If that was so, Mr Kinray thought, then it was probably his fault and not Zoe's. He'd always given the girl the impression there was no other clock quite like St Mary's. Well, perhaps it was time to satisfy her curiosity before it reached bursting point. After all, Zoe was nine now and a sensible lass.

Somewhere in the distance, Mr Kinray heard the hee-haw, hee-haw of an ambulance siren.

"Somebody's in trouble," he muttered to himself.

3 Warning

THE RED LIGHT glowed in the studio.
They had to sit still and keep quiet
when the red light was on, indicating
they were 'on air'. They sat in the usual
circle, Penny holding out the hand
microphone to Sam who was reading
the 'Messages in the Bottle'. These
were news items about what was
happening in the Roundbay Radio area
over the next week, especially things
that would be of interest to children.
Because Penny and the Crew were
supposed to be 'on an island' in the
programme, the information was supposed to 'arrive in a bottle that's been

washed ashore'.

The Island was Penny Cruso's idea,
suggested by her own name. Donald
thought it a clever one, especially the
introduction of Friday the 'parrot'.
This, like the seagulls and the sound of
waves, was provided by a tape. It was
played by Greg Wills who was 'driving'

the show in the next room.

Donald could see Greg the other side
of a large glass window, surrounded by
an array of sliding levers, switches,
leads and turntables, besides tapes and
records. It was all necessary to keep
even a fairly straightforward programme like *Cruso's Island* on the air.

The red light went out when Sam finished speaking and an advertising jingle burst into life. They all relaxed.

"Right," Penny said. "That just leaves us time for the last record. Who has the last request?"

"Me," Donald said.

After the programme was over, they all went out into the main office. More of the desks were filled now and there was a clatter of typewriters.

"Thanks, all of you," Penny said. "Super programme. Donald, if you hang on a minute I'll find that book I want you to review next Saturday."

"Right," Donald said.

Sam and Tracy went towards the stairs while Donald followed Penny to her desk.

The Programme Controller was waiting for them.

"Ah, Penny," Mr Munford said. "Have you a moment?"

"Yes, of course." Donald noticed the anxious look flicker across Penny's face. He hovered in the background.

"Quite a good show this morning," Mr Munford said with a thin, tight smile.

"I think we need at least one more crew member," Penny began.

"*Quite* good," Mr Munford repeated. He paused. Some of the noise in the office seemed to have died away. "But I think there's room for improvement, don't you?"

"Well – yes." Penny's face became flushed.

"Every programme must contribute," Mr Munford said.

Donald watched him. The skin seemed to have been stretched tightly across the man's cheekbones so that his mouth seemed to find it difficult to do anything but remain in that fixed smile. Yet it wasn't a nice smile.

"Every programme must be at its best – or come off the air," the Programme Controller said. The sentence hung like a thunder cloud. "In fact, I'm not even sure Roundbay Radio *needs* a children's programme at all. It does take up valuable broadcasting time."

"Oh, but it's becoming very popular," Penny protested. "We get lots of letters –"

"From children." Mr Munford made them sound like nasty things that crawled out of duck ponds. "But is a children's programme important? I need convincing that it is." And the Programme Controller swung round and headed back towards his office.

"Oh dear," Penny said. "I didn't like the sound of that, Donald."

Neither did Donald. He called Mr Munford a rude name under his breath.

After Penny had given him the book she wanted him to review, he went down to the reception area. In one corner a speaker played Roundbay Radio programmes continously. Donald heard Greg Wills making some special announcement over the air.

" . . . and a number of these canisters have been found on the beach this morning. Police and firemen are searching the seafront as they fear others may have been washed ashore during last night's storm. The canisters are thought to have come from a ship which was wrecked earlier this month and which sank twenty miles down the Channel. The public are warned that the contents of the canisters are dangerous if exposed to the air. The fumes

can make you ill, and already two workmen
and a fisherman have been taken to Auksea
General Hospital for treatment . . ."

Donald went out of the swing doors.
No stroll along the beach this afternoon, he thought.

Zoe's arm ached from the weight of the
sack.

She had reached a flight of stone
steps which led to an alleyway at the
top of the town. She sat on the top step,
breathing heavily. She still had the
horrible taste in her mouth.

It was the quiet end of Auksea, the
streets dingier, the buildings shabbier.
Zoe stretched her legs in front of her.
There was something she planned to do
before taking her collection of bits and
pieces to the man. She put her hand in
her anorak pocket. Her fingers touched

a hard metal object inside and her heartbeat quickened as she drew it out.

It was a large black key.

Like a dragon's tooth, she thought, fanciful for a moment.

Then St Mary's clock struck and she jumped to her feet, her conscience catching her by surprise.

Donald cycled round the small knot of people who had gathered on the cliff road, all staring down at the beach. Police and firemen were searching for the canisters below. Donald remembered Greg Wills' warning.

Greg Wills – now there was a chap he envied, Donald thought as he got off his bike and stared with the others at the activity beneath him. One day *he* would be a reporter and presenter like Greg Wills. *Cruso's Island* was good training, but one day . . .

Yet, after hearing Mr Munford earlier, Donald wondered how long the children's programme – and himself with it – would stay on the air. He had the horrible feeling his broadcasting career was about to be cut short.

A man had come to stand beside him, looking down at the beach.

"Never know what the sea's going to throw up these days," the man said, shaking his head. He was tall, about the same age as Donald's father, and his tanned face was almost completely surrounded by ginger hair, the curls on his head matching his whiskers. He wore a thick polo-necked sweater and paint-splattered jeans.

"Let's hope they find all the canisters," Donald said. "They sound dangerous."

The man turned and looked sharply at him. "I know that voice," he said. "Don't I?"

Donald felt his face burn, but couldn't help being pleased.

The man smiled. "Thought so. You're Donald, from *Cruso's Island*, aren't you?"

Donald nodded and grinned.

"I'm good at voices," the man said. "And I always listen to *Cruso's Island*, it's an excellent programme."

Donald wished Mr Munford had been able to hear that remark. "You don't mind it being a children's programme?"

"Why should I?" The man looked surprised by the question. "Anyway, I

know a bit about islands – real ones, I
mean." He seemed about to go on but
then suddenly pointed to the beach.
"Looks like they've found another."

Donald saw a uniformed policeman
holding an orange object above his
head. The policeman, like the other
searchers, was wearing some sort of
mask across the lower part of his face,
covering his mouth and nose.

"At least it looks in one piece," the man beside Donald said. "It's when they're broken that they're dangerous."

It was something about the solitariness of the figure, standing there slightly stooped, that reminded Donald. He had completely forgotten the girl until that moment, but now a picture flashed in and out of his mind, like a torch beam being switched on and off. Something must have shown in his face.

"What is it?" the man said.

"I've just remembered something," Donald told him. "*Somebody*, rather." He explained about the girl he had seen beachcombing on his way to the Studios that morning.

"Of course, she may not have found anything at all," Donald said. "Or if she did, she may have handed it in by now."

The man frowned. "Then again, maybe she hasn't. Girl, you say? What did she look like?"

"Smallish," Donald said. "About eight or nine, I should think. She had a blue anorak and short fair hair."

The man looked up quickly. "Short fair hair?"

"What's the matter? Do you know her?"

"Not exactly," the man said. "But I have a feeling she might have been collecting things for *me*."

4   Up the Tower

THERE WAS A wide flight of steps which led to St Mary's church, but there was another way as well. A narrow path led from an alleyway behind the shops and along the edge of a small sloping graveyard. It was the path Mr Kinray used when he went to wind the clock.

It was the path Zoe used now.

It led to a side entrance with an arched porch and a heavy oak door with a huge ring handle the size of a pramwheel. Zoe caught hold of it and there was a giant CLICK from the latch the other side.

She pushed the door open.

Inside, it was like shutting out the

world. A cool, silent island, only the echo of Zoe's feet against the flagstoned floor. She moved quickly between the empty pews, up the centre of the aisle to where some stone steps led to a curtained section.

She parted the curtains and peered into a square area where bellropes came down through holes in the ceiling and were draped back from the centre and tied to hooks on the wall. Like an unwound maypole awaiting children.

It was here that Zoe had often waited while her grandfather had gone up the tower to wind the clock. A frustrated Zoe had squatted impatiently on the floor until Mr Kinray had returned, locking the small arched door which led to the tower stairs and pocketing the key.

It was this key which Zoe took from

her anorak pocket now.

It fitted snugly into the lock. She turned it – and the door creaked open to reveal the first few steps to the tower. Zoe left the sack outside and stepped in.

The steps had been hollowed out at the centre by thousands of feet over the years. Against the wall was a handrail made of old bell ropes. It was a narrow stairway and Zoe was surprised her grandfather didn't get stuck.

She passed slit windows, some with diamond-shaped panes, others with no glass at all. Shafts of daylight cut through, showing up the cracks in the wall.

Up and up, round and round.

And then she found herself at the back of St Mary's church clock.

It was not what she'd expected. For one thing, the workings seemed to take up the biggest part of the square room in which she was now standing. They stretched along one wall, wheels turning, weights moving, small cogs knitting in with bigger cogs, and the large swinging arm of the pendulum with its great heavy base moving back and forth, back and forth.

The workings were fixed at a height taller than Zoe and she had to stand on tiptoe to see it properly. The pendulum

swung underneath in an open space.

The room smelled of oil and Zoe saw that each part was kept beautifully clean. Then, after staring at the clock for some minutes, she moved out of the little room and ventured up the rest of the stairs.

They led to the bell tower. She would stay a bit longer, then she'd go down again. There was still the sack of stuff to get to the man and she didn't want to be too late back at her grandfather's shop in case he suddenly took a fit in his head to look for the tower key.

Zoe didn't like to admit it, but the clock had not been as exciting as she'd expected. Also, she was rather frightened of the empty silence of the tower. Yes, she'd clear off in a minute.

Miss Forrester opened the main door of

St Mary's church and walked directly to the curtained area at the back. In one hand, she carried a suitcase.

Reaching the curtains, she put down the suitcase and collected a chair from the corner. This she placed beneath the curtain rail and, taking great care, climbed up on to it.

Miss Forrester began to remove the curtain from the rail, her fingers slipping deftly over the nylon hooks.

"These ought to have been cleaned months ago," she said to herself. Miss Forrester liked things neat and tidy. She worked quickly, finally folding up the curtains and putting them in the suitcase.

It was only then she noticed the open door leading to the tower; and then the small sack outside.

"How extraordinary," Miss Forrester

said. She went to the doorway and peered upwards. "Mr Kinray? Are you up there?"

There was no reply. Yet she *thought* she heard a slight movement above. Most odd. And worrying. The door was always locked unless the old man was attending to the clock. Could he have gone up and been taken ill?

Making a sudden decision, Miss Forrester began to climb the stairs. Although she would not have admitted it, she was a little nervous. Suppose she found the old man dead beside his precious clock?

But then she was in the little square room with the clock workings and feeling weak with relief at finding it empty. There was always the bell tower, of course, but what would Mr Kinray be doing up there? However, having come this far it would be as well to check.

She made the climb up the remainder of the stairs and peered across the top of the huge bells. It was difficult to see much in the dim light, but there was nowhere a man the size of Mr Kinray could possible be hidden from view.

Miss Forrester went back down to the church. It was obvious what had happened, she told herself. Mr Kinray had forgotten to lock up after winding the clock the previous night. Well, for safety's sake, she would lock up for him and take the key to the bookshop when she was passing later.

And then there was this sack.

Miss Forrester peered inside and wrinkled her nose. It smelled seaweedy. But it was obviously not the sort of thing to be left lying around in the church. She would put it with the other

rubbish where it belonged.

Miss Forrester slammed the tower door and locked it. Then, sack in one hand and suitcase in the other, she walked back down the aisle. She was humming 'All Things Bright and Beautiful' by the time she got outside.

Zoe, crouching behind the large tenor bell, heard the sound of the tower door being closed, the key turning in the lock.

"Oh, no!" she cried, but her voice was little more than a whisper. A sickly feeling swept over her like a great hot wave and, surprised to find her face wet, she wiped tears from her cheeks.

Then she remembered her sack.

5   *Donald's Idea*

THE WIND BLEW through the man's
ginger whiskers and mass of ginger
hair. A look of deep concern creased his
face.

"We'd better let the police know," he
said. "Just in case."

Donald nodded. "You don't know
her name though?"

"No, afraid not. Even so, the descrip-
tion . . ." His voice tailed off.

"But why was she collecting things
from the beach for you?" Donald asked.
"*What* was she collecting?"

"Probably driftwood, bottles, tin
cans." The man saw Donald's puzzled
expression and explained. "I'm a

59

painter, you see. At least, I'm trying to be. I'm interested in shapes, colours, that sort of thing. Well, it was just before Christmas when I was walking along the beach and saw this small girl. She had just picked up a long, beautifully shaped piece of cuttlefish."

Donald began to see. "And you wanted it to paint?"

"To draw, actually. I saw at once it would make a splendid subject, and I asked her if she'd let me have it. She seemed a bit put out, but then I offered to buy it for a few pence. She perked up at that. 'All right,' she said. 'How about anything else interesting that I find?' So I laughed and told her, all right, if it was something I could use, I'd pay her for it."

"Did she find anything else?"

"Yes. A few days later, she turned up

at my cottage with some bits and pieces. I paid her for them and she seemed delighted. She'd do it again, she said, when she next visited Auksea."

"She's not a local kid then?" Donald said.

"I'd guess not," the painter said. He looked farther along the cliff road where a black-and-white police car stood beside the verge. A uniformed police-man in a peaked cap was leaning

against the bonnet. "Look, I think I'll just go and mention this to him."

Donald watched as the bearded man explained things to the policeman, pointing back at Donald once or twice. Then he saw the policeman get into the car and use his radio, speaking into a microphone. After a few minutes, the painter returned.

"He's put a call through to the local police station," he told Donald. "As far as they know, no girl has reported picking up one of the canisters. Even so, it's possible she may have one and not be aware that it's dangerous. So they're going to begin looking for her."

"That could take ages," Donald said.

The painter nodded, looking worried again. "And by the time they find her, it might be too late. Still, if she was collecting the things for me, she might

have gone to my cottage. I think I'll go
and see. Coming?"

"OK," Donald said. He felt involved,
being the one to have seen the girl in the
first place.

The painter's cottage was down an
unmade road off the clifftop. It led
nowhere except to four ancient cottages
set in a semi-circle. The man led the
way to one at the end. It looked slightly
run down. Under a lean-to at the side
of the building was a small dinghy on a
trailer.

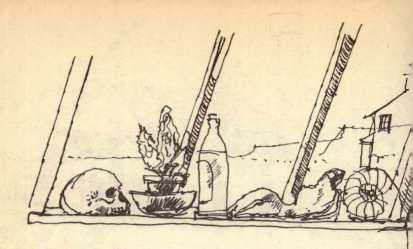

"Come on in," the man said. "By the way, my name's Paul Fretzer."

Donald stepped into the cottage and found himself immediately in the living room. An open staircase twisted upwards in one corner.

"My studio's upstairs, want to see?" Paul Fretzer led the way.

It was really an attic with a slanting window in the roof. There was a cluttered bench at one end, but everywhere else the walls and floor were covered in paintings and drawings. Some were of

Auksea, others of more ordinary objects like driftwood tangled with seaweed or a chunk of rock.

"They are very good," Donald said. "Have you been a painter long?"

"For as long as I can remember, although it's only the last year or so I've tried making a living by it." He sighed. "I suppose we'll just have to sit and wait for our young friend."

Donald could tell he was worried. "I was thinking," Donald said. "Even if she isn't local, some other kid will probably know her, have got friendly when she comes to stay."

"The police will probably think of that," Paul Fretzer said. "I expect they'll ask the children who live around here."

"That'll take some time," Donald said. "And the girl might be in danger if the canister – if she's got one – accidentally breaks open."

"True," the painter said. "But the police don't have an unlimited supply of men."

"There's another way," Donald said, becoming more excited as the thought grew. "I've just had this idea. I think I'll nip back to the Studios."

A boy called Vic Farley rubbed the grass-stain off his cricket ball. He polished it against the side of his jeans, then threw it into the air and caught it on the run.

"Better," he said to himself. He was improving.

"You want to play in Molton Street cricket team, you gotta learn to throw and catch," Nicky Lacey had told him.

"He'll be too old to play anything by

then," Kevin Yates had said. "He'll be an old age pensioner."

They made fun of him all the time, Vic was used to that. He was seven, whereas all the others were ten or more. But he'd show them.

He threw the ball at the hedge which divided the patch of grass where he was playing from St Mary's churchyard the other side. The ball went over the hedge and smacked into a sack of rubbish beside some dustbins and a pile of dead flowers. A little earlier, Vic had seen a woman bring the sack from the church.

It had fallen over and some of the contents had spilled out. Vic went across, scrambling through one of the many gaps in the hedge. The ball was next to a bright orange tin with strange, foreign-looking writing on it. Vic threw the tin up in the air and caught it.

He looked at it. It would make a smashing target, he decided. He threw it into the air again, but this time missed it when it came down. When he picked it up, there was a dent in one side.

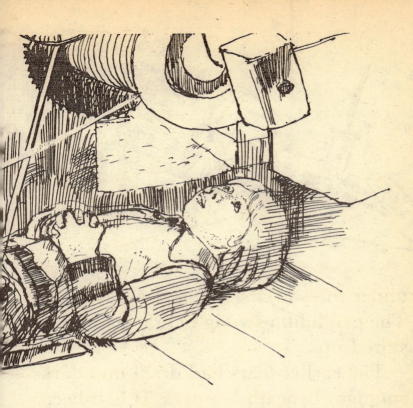

Zoe sat in the square room and stared
moodily at the clock workings. The
sickly-feeling had passed over, but there
was still the horrible taste in her mouth.

She watched the wheels moving, the
pendulum swinging beneath. For something to do, she crawled over and slid

under the workings, lying on her back.
The pendulum swung beside her as she
stared up.

The earlier tears had dried into dark
smudges beneath her eyes. It had been
crazy coming here, she could see that
now. Taking the key, sneaking up here,
and now getting herself locked in. And
it hadn't been worth it. The clock had
been a great disappointment.

And now what? Wait until whoever
had locked her in came back? *If* they

came back. Or would they take the key to her grandfather? What would the old man say?

After a while, she eased herself out from under the workings. As she pulled the top part of her body clear, her foot brushed against the pendulum. But she didn't notice.

Zoe went down the stairs, her legs wobbly and a faintness which made her feel as though she was spinning.

"Hey!" she shouted. "Anybody there?"

She hadn't looked back when she left the little square room. She hadn't seen the long arm of the pendulum gradually slowing in its back-and-forth movement.

She hadn't seen it stop.

6   Special Broadcast

"RIGHT, NOW WHILE that record was playing, Penny Cruso popped into the studio. Hi, Penny, what can I do for you?"

"Hallo, Greg. I have a special message for all Cruso's Island listeners and to any other children who might be tuned in. We want to contact a young girl who was on the beach this morning and who may have picked up one of those dangerous canisters you've been warning about, Greg. We don't think she comes from Auksea but that she's staying with friends or relatives. Donald, who saw her earlier, will describe her. Go ahead, Donald."

"She's about nine years old, smallish with short fair hair, and wearing a blue anorak. She may also be carrying a small sack."

"Thanks, Donald. So if you know this girl or have seen her, please call in or phone us, or go to your nearest police station and mention this broadcast."

Mr Kinray glanced at St Mary's clock. Twenty past eleven. Zoe ought to be back by now. He felt a small stirring of unease. After all, he was responsible for the girl.

He picked up a book about wild flowers, turning the pages but not seeing the illustrations. Where *was* she? After some minutes, he snatched at the net curtain and looked at St Mary's clock again.

Twenty past eleven.

Mr Kinray blinked. "It's stopped," he said, as if the world had stopped turning.

He heaved himself from his chair and

headed for the hook under the stairs where he kept the tower key. And it was then that Mr Kinray received another shock.

The key wasn't there.

Mr Kinray stared at the empty hook, as if by doing so it might make the key reappear. Then he said, *"Zoe?"* and went to pull down the CLOSED sign on the shop door.

"I heard the broadcast," the boy said.

They were in the reception hall of
Roundbay Radio – Donald, Penny and
a boy about Donald's age. The boy was
wearing jodphurs, a riding hat and a
bright red sweater.

"I was on my way to riding school," the boy went on. "Mum had the car radio on."

Penny nodded. "And the girl?"

"Well, it *sounds* like the one who comes to stay with Mr Kinray. Her name is Zoe."

"Mr Kinray keeps the second-hand bookshop on the hill near St Mary's church," Donald told Penny.

The boy nodded. "That's the one. She's Mr Kinray's grand-daughter. I think she's staying with him at the moment."

After the boy had gone, Penny phoned the bookshop.

"There's no reply," she said.

"Odd," Donald said. "His shop is always open on Saturdays."

"Perhaps you'd better go and take a look. I'll wait here in case there are any

more messages."

Miss Forrester arrived at the book-shop at the same time as Donald. She had planned to return the tower key.

"It's closed," she said. "Most peculiar."

"Have you seen his grand-daughter?" Donald asked. He felt a sense of alarm growing within him.

"Zoe?" Miss Forrester said. "Is she visiting? Perhaps they've gone out for the day. It doesn't explain the clock tower being unlocked though."

"Clock tower?" Donald repeated.

Miss Forrester explained how she'd found the tower door open, the key in the lock. "And a sack of rubbish, of all things," she finished.

"What did you do with it?" Donald asked, his skin suddenly prickly with excitement.

"I put it with the rest of the rubbish at the back of the church. I couldn't just – wait a moment, where are you going?" Miss Forrester stared after Donald's retreating figure as he ran up the hill towards the church.

He saw the sack as he ran along the

side of the church. It was amongst the pile of grass cuttings and dead flowers. Donald immediately slowed up, sniffing gently.

No peculiar smell, but he couldn't be too careful.

He saw the jumble of shells, driftwood and polythene bottles. Gingerly, he began to sort through.

After only a few moments, he knew

the canister wasn't there.

"So where is it?" Donald said.

There was a boy in the field at the back of the churchyard, Donald noticed out of the corner of his eye. He saw the boy collect a ball from the hedge and make his way back to the centre of the grass.

Donald looked up at St Mary's clock to check the time. Twenty past eleven?

"It's stopped," Donald said, frowning. "Now *that's* odd as well."

He began to walk towards the church to investigate, passing the hedge which divided the churchyard from the field. Over the top, he saw the boy with the ball take aim.

At first Donald thought the boy was aiming at him, then he saw the target, sitting on a dead tree branch amongst the tall grass.

Something orange.

Donald pushed through a gap in the hedge and ran.

Vic took aim, one eye half closed. As he threw, there was a shout from somewhere. Out of the corner of his eye, Vic saw the moving figure of Donald.

"Hey, what are you doing!"

Vic was furious. It was his best throw yet. For the first time the ball had been right on target, sailing across the grass, when a hand reached out from nowhere and snatched it from the air.

7   Final Report

"AND NOW A round-up of the local news. Police say they think they have now recovered all the canisters washed up by last night's storm. This includes the one picked up by a nine-year-old girl early this morning. As a result of broadcasts by our own Penny Cruso and Cruso's Island crew member, Donald Bilsby, the girl was traced before any harm came to her or others. This afternoon, police thanked Roundbay Radio, and Donald and Penny in particular, for their help. It was a young listener who set them on the right track . . ."

Penny Cruso smiled as Donald came into the Roundbay Radio offices.

"You're famous, Donald, did you hear?"

Donald grinned back. "How's the girl Zoe, have you heard?"

"Much better," Penny said. "I

phoned her grandfather. She went to the hospital for a check-up and they're keeping her in overnight, just to be sure there are no more ill effects. She was lucky. She wasn't as close to the damaged canister as that fisherman and the two workmen."

"I still don't understand how she came to be in St Mary's tower."

"She borrowed her grandfather's key," Penny said. "Mr Kinray was telling me. Then Miss Forrester accidentally locked her in."

"Oh," Donald said.

"It was Miss Forrester who let Zoe out again," Penny said. "She followed you up the hill from the bookshop after you raced off to look for the sack."

Donald nodded. "I know, I saw her afterwards. And Mr Kinray was in the church. They'd both noticed that the clock had stopped."

"Apparently, Zoe did that without realising it," Penny said.

Donald sat down in a chair by Penny's desk. It was still only mid-afternoon yet so much had happened that he seemed to have been up for hours and hours.

"I've just come from that painter chap's cottage," Donald said. "I thought I'd better drop in and let him know what was happening. He was worried."

"You know who he is, don't you?" Penny said.

Donald frowned. "He's Paul Fretzer, a painter."

"He's also Paul Fretzer, round-the-world yachtsman of a few years ago," Penny told him.

"Round-the-world-? Really! Come to

think of it, he said something about knowing some real islands when he was talking about *Cruso's Island*."

"Did he now?" Penny said. "That's interesting. He would make a good guest for the programme. You could interview him, Donald."

"If we still have a programme," Donald said gloomily. He looked across to Mr Munford's office, but the Programme Controller wasn't there.

Penny smiled. "Oh, we have a programme all right. That's one thing today has proved. Roundbay Radio needs listeners of *all* ages. Even Mr Munford had to admit that before he left earlier."

"He did?"

"He did indeed. *Cruso's Island* looks like running for a long, long time," Penny said.

And it did.

FOR THE BEST IN PAPERBACKS, LOOK FOR THE

In every corner of the world, on every subject under the sun, Penguin represents quality and variety – the very best in publishing today.

For complete information about books available from Penguin – including Pelicans, Puffins, Peregrines and Penguin Classics – and how to order them, write to us at the appropriate address below. Please note that for copyright reasons the selection of books varies from country to country.

In the United Kingdom: For a complete list of books available from Penguin in the U.K., please write to *Dept E.P., Penguin Books Ltd, Harmondsworth, Middlesex, UB7 0DA*

In the United States: For a complete list of books available from Penguin in the U.S., please write to *Dept BA, Penguin, 299 Murray Hill Parkway, East Rutherford, New Jersey 07073*

In Canada: For a complete list of books available from Penguin in Canada, please write to *Penguin Books Canada Ltd, 2801 John Street, Markham, Ontario L3R 1B4*

In Australia: For a complete list of books available from Penguin in Australia, please write to the *Marketing Department, Penguin Books Australia Ltd, P.O. Box 257, Ringwood, Victoria 3134*

In New Zealand: For a complete list of books available from Penguin in New Zealand, please write to the *Marketing Department, Penguin Books (NZ) Ltd, Private Bag, Takapuna, Auckland 9*

In India: For a complete list of books available from Penguin, please write to *Penguin Overseas Ltd, 706 Eros Apartments, 56 Nehru Place, New Delhi, 110019*

In Holland: For a complete list of books available from Penguin in Holland, please write to *Penguin Books Nederland B.V., Postbus 195, NL–1380AD Weesp, Netherlands*

In Germany: For a complete list of books available from Penguin, please write to *Penguin Books Ltd, Friedrichstrasse 10 – 12, D–6000 Frankfurt Main 1, Federal Republic of Germany*

In Spain: For a complete list of books available from Penguin in Spain, please write to *Longman Penguin España, Calle San Nicolas 15, E–28013 Madrid, Spain*